Track that Scat!

Written by **Lisa Morlock**   Illustrated by **Carrie Anne Bradshaw**

To Will and Emma, who have nature in their souls.

—Lisa

For my Lily Annabelle—you make each day an adventure.

—Carrie Anne

Special Thanks

*The author extends a special thank-you to Cindy Blobaum,
naturalist, educator, and writer, for her animal expertise.*

Text Copyright © 2012 Lisa Morlock
Illustration Copyright © 2012 Carrie Anne Bradshaw

All rights reserved. No part of this book may be reproduced in any manner
without the express written consent of the publisher, except in the case of brief
excerpts in critical reviews and articles. All inquiries should be addressed to:

Sleeping Bear Press®
315 E. Eisenhower Parkway, Suite 200
Ann Arbor, MI 48108
www.sleepingbearpress.com

Sleeping Bear Press is an imprint of Gale, a part of Cengage Learning.

10 9 8 7 6 5 4 3 2 1

Printed by China Translation & Printing Services Limited,
Guangdong Province, China. 1st printing. 10/2011

Library of Congress Cataloging-in-Publication Data

Morlock, Lisa, 1969-
Track that scat! / written by Lisa Morlock ;
illustrated by Carrie Anne Bradshaw.
p. cm.
ISBN 978-1-58536-536-4
1. Animal droppings—Juvenile literature.
2. Animal tracks—Juvenile literature.
I. Bradshaw, Carrie Anne. II. Title.
QL768.M667 2012
591.47'9—dc23   2011028148

Warning: Watch Your Step!

To learn which animals live in your area, search for clues on the ground. If you look closely, you're bound to find footprints known as **TRACKS**. Every animal leaves a different set of tracks behind. These tracks are easy to see in mud or snow. If you find tracks, there is probably **SCAT** close by. Scat, also known as poop, can be used to help identify an animal and what it eats. Whether you're playing in the backyard, exploring a city pond, or visiting a state park, clues about the woodland creatures in this book may be right under your feet.

Scat: Defined

What is **scat**? The word has several definitions, and each is used in this story.

1. Definition: **to go off quickly; to move fast**
Part of speech: verb
Origin: interjection used to drive away a cat; 1838

2. Definition: **animal fecal droppings**
Part of speech: noun
Origin: from the Greek **skat-** or **skor**, excrement; 1927

3. Definition: **(n) jazz singing with nonsense syllables; (vi) to improvise nonsense syllables to an instrumental accompaniment**
Parts of speech: noun, verb Intransitive
Origin: unknown; 1929

Finn ties new boots on restless feet.
"Skit-scat," says Mom. "Do keep them neat."
"Sure 'nuff," Finn says as she leaves home.
But Mom knows toes are made to roam.

Finn yells as she flings wide the door,

"Come on, Skeeter. Let's go explore!"
But...what? That lazy hound won't go.
Finn nudges him with a big
heave-ho.

So fancy-free, the two hightail
past pellets on the grassy trail.

Zigzagging tracks in broad V clumps,
whatever hurried through here **JUMPS!**

With one trip-slip,
Finn's foot goes **splat**.

Oh no!
Right into...

...rabbit scat!

"Eeek-eeek!" is all she has to say
before she bunny-hops away.

Eastern Cottontail Rabbits

To follow a rabbit's tracks, let its hind legs lead you. Bounding at 15 miles per hour, front paws hit the ground as larger hind paws swing forward and land just ahead of the front ones. The rabbit remains coiled up like a spring until it pushes off with powerful back legs. Momentarily, it's completely airborne. The rabbit's movement resembles what we do when playing leapfrog.

Rabbits eat their own poop. When their scat comes out the first time, it's in soft, moist pellets. The animal eats these pellets. The second time, the pellets are dry and rounded with a flat side, and found in piles or as scattered singles.

Rabbits typically are silent animals, but they can growl, hiss, or make a purr-like sound. When in danger, rabbits have a squeal that can sound similar to a child's scream.

Tracks *Hind* *Fore* Scat

Finn leaps across a winding creek.
Now Skeeter's playing hide-and-seek.

Finn looks around. What does she spy?
A green grass patty mixed with rye.

Three-toed web prints grouped together.
Nearby floats a long tail feather.

With one trop-plop,
Finn's foot goes **splat**.
Oh no!
She steps into...

...goose scat!

"Honk-honk!" is all Finn has to say.
She flaps her arms and flies away.

Canada Geese

To find Canada goose tracks, look near
water. They have three toes connected
by a web. At the end of each toe is a wide,
blunt claw. Their webbed feet make it easy
for them to swim.

A Canada goose produces 1 to 3 pounds of sausage-
shaped scat every day! That's quite a bit of poop for a bird
that weighs around 10 pounds. Geese are herbivores and eat
water plants, grasses, and grains. Due to this diet, fresh goose
scat is a greenish gray that darkens over time.

Geese honk when migrating, but they're also famous for hissing
when something threatens them or their nests.

Scat   Tracks

Finn lands upon a hollow log.
And yells, "Come on!" to that old dog.

Five-toed tracks, like handprints—see?
A messy pile beneath the tree.

A den! Her hound plays show-and-smell—
dry leaves, fish bones, a walnut shell.

With one tromp-stomp
Finn's foot goes **splat**.
Oh no!
Right into...

...raccoon scat!

"Growl-growl," is all Finn has to say.
Like a bandit, she steals away.

Raccoons

Raccoons have front paws that look like small hands and back paws that resemble feet with very long toes. Their paws end with a fat, round heel, and their toes end with long claws. Raccoons shuffle when they walk, scuffing the ground with their back feet.

A raccoon makes its own toilet, called a latrine, close to its den. Raccoons also leave piles of scat on rocks and fallen logs. The scat is blackish brown with a reddish tint and forms a crumbly, segmented cylinder with flat ends. Never pick up any scat, but especially not raccoon scat, as it often contains a dangerous roundworm parasite that can make people very sick.

Raccoons make a calm coo-like sound. When upset, they chatter, snarl, and growl. They'll also hiss as a warning and make a purr-like sound when content.

Tracks

Fore *Hind*

Scat

Finn shuffles past another track.
Toes form a line from front to back.
A pinch of fur, a feather, too.
Mystery seeds and tail of shrew.

With one slid-skid
Finn's foot goes **splat**.
Oh no!
She's stepped in...

...red fox scat.

"Snort-snarl!" is all Finn has to say,
And then she foxtrots straight away.

Red Foxes

When they walk, red foxes place one foot directly in front of the other, leaving a straight line of tracks. They walk this way because their chest cavity is very narrow. Each paw forms a small oval shape with four clawed toes, and their heel pads make a broad V-shape.

Red fox scat is about as thick as an adult's thumb and twice as long. In winter, their scat is often covered with an outer layer of fur tangled around small bones and may be rope-shaped, tapered, and segmented. In the summer, there may be seeds or green plant material present, and the scat will be crumbly with blunt ends.

Red foxes are usually quiet, but their bark sounds similar to that of a yappy dog. If in danger, they let out a sharp shriek. They also growl and whine.

Tracks   *Fore*   *Hind*   Scat

Finn bounds until she sees clawed ground
with scratchy dig marks all around.
Five oval toes form little paws
and five clear points define front claws.

A small black pile of smashed turtle eggs,
bumblebee wings, and spider legs.

A rotten odor rushes through.
Finn says, **"Hey, Skeeter, is that you?"**
Suddenly Skeeter rockets past.
That dog has never run so fast.

A white-striped streak, tail-raising funk.
Oh no!
This scat belongs to...

Tracks

Fore

Hind

Scat

Striped Skunks

Skunks leave five-toed front and back prints. Each paw
comes with a set of claws the skunk uses to dig up food.
Their back prints are larger and set wider than their front prints,
because they walk with a waddle.

If there's a small scat pile with insect wings, legs, and other parts sticking out, it was
likely left by a skunk. Skunk scat narrows at one or both ends and is about three inches long.

As far as a skunk is concerned, people should fear the rear. Before they spray, skunks usually
hiss or snarl a warning. They'll do something like a handstand to align their bottoms with an enemy's
face. Skunks can spray a target from 15 feet away. When they spray, a choking mist fills a 30-foot
circle around the animal.

SKUNK!

"Pee-uw!" is all Finn has to say.
Nose plugged, she sprints to get away.

Finn slows below a chickadee
that's singing in a maple tree.

The bird takes flight. Finn feels a **splat**.
New boots are blotched by songbird scat.

A twirl of black, a whitish ring.
The only thing to do is…

Black-capped Chickadees

Chickadees have three toes that face forward like the tines of a fork and one toe that stretches straight back, but these tiny birds leave virtually no detectable tracks.

Hold two quarters in your hand, and you'll have an idea of how much a chickadee weighs. Yet, this little song bird eats at almost every moment of the day, so it poops a lot. When fresh, its scat looks like a small round pile of pencil lead.

Chickadees use lots of calls to talk to each other, but the easiest way to detect them is to listen for the "chick-a-dee-dee-dee" sound they make.

Tracks   Scat

Chick-a-
dee-dee-dee.
What a day!
In brand new boots, she scats away.

Fresh woodsy air, relaxing stroll,
oh, Finn's got nature in her soul...
and on her sole,
around her sole,
beneath her sole.

Ring-a-ling!
Mom sounds the bell.
Time to go home—it's just as well.
That dog is tired.
His tail has drooped.
Both Skeeter and Finn's boots are pooped.